FADED MEMORIES

A NIGHT SHIFT NOVELLA

NIGHT SHIFT
BOOK 3

CHRISTINA C. JONES

D1715453

WARM HUES CREATIVE

ONE

I wasn't in a very *cheery* mood.

Despite my best efforts otherwise.

Christmas Eve normally found me at my merry-and-brightest, but I couldn't seem to find any of that usual energy to keep me pushing through the endless stream of customers augmenting their own moods with liquor.

If I had to make one more *Mistletoe Mule,* I was going to scream.

Not really.

But, I cursed the lack of foresight in my lively agreement to work the bar — on *Christmas Eve* of all nights — a little more with every cute metal cup with the *Night Shift* logo on it I dropped to the counter in front of me.

Ice.

Vodka.

Lime Juice.

Laken's precious hard ginger beer.

Cranberry juice.

Stupid mini candy cane on the side.

"You should try to look a little more sullen," Lark teased as she came to a nearby register to cash a ticket out. "Really drive home the *cranky bartender* on Christmas vibe."

"I'm giving a vibe?" I questioned with wide eyes — a response that garnered a raised eyebrow from my cousin.

"You're joking, right?" she finished what she was doing, then grabbed the receipt and a nearby pen before turning to walk away. "You've been in a mood all week..."

Really?

Shit.

And here I'd been thinking I was doing at least a *decent* job of hiding it.

My arrival in Blackwood hadn't been timed with the holidays, but they'd certainly been a potent factor in what some — my parents — called a *snap decision to run off across the world.*

As if there weren't any nonstop flights between here and New Orleans.

I could admit that I'd hated to uproot my life – if we could even call it that – with very little explanation or preparation, but when one of my favorite cousins got the inkling I needed a change of space and pace and offered me a job, it had taken little thought to accept.

Hell, I didn't even think about it.

I just said *yes,* cause the thinking had already happened. I couldn't take another round of holidays like last year.

Last year was a damn disaster.

And this year hadn't been shaping up to be much better emotionally until I bought the plane ticket I hoped was going to bring a major shift to my life. I'd felt such immediate relief stepping into *Night Shift* that first day, fresh off my flight, that it was a bit jarring to hear *you've been in a mood since you arrived.*

"How's this?" I asked Lark when she came back, after I'd loaded one of the server's trays with tonight's signature cocktail. I put on my biggest smile, and Lark's eyes went wide.

"Babe... it's fucking terrifying," she said, so solemnly that I immediately put my teeth back in my mouth.

And then we both broke into laughter.

"Why would you say that?!" I asked once I'd regained a bit of composure.

"Because I like to deal in the *truth,*" she laughed, stepping in closer to meet my gaze. "Don't do that shit ever again in your life."

"In life?"

"*In life,*" she giggled, then dipped her head to ask, "Hey, seriously though... you good?"

"Yes," I swore, putting a hand to my chest. "It's just... you know..."

She groaned, pulling me into a hug. "Yeah, I do. Fuck him for ruining everything for you."

Everything covered a lot, unfortunately, but I knew that right now she was mostly referring to my usual enjoyment of the holiday season. Since childhood, I'd been very much a *Holly Jolly Christmas* kinda chick, to the point of annoyance for friends and family.

The *him* was my ex-husband, who'd absolutely bested me in one last act of pettiness – having me served at the office party on Christmas Eve – the party I *planned* — when I hadn't even realized my marriage was in *that* much trouble.

It was frighteningly vindictive.

And disastrously *effective.*

His goal had been maximum emotional damage, and he absolutely achieved it – months and months later, not only was I damn near dreading the winter holiday season, I was still getting pity stares at the office – a *big* reason behind me finally saying *fuck it* and moving to Blackwood on a whim.

I was the Kimble.

Making *Kimble Bourbon Co.* **my** family's business, over generations.

I shouldn't be the one feeling awkward and out of place at work, *he* should.

Instead, he was still welcome with open arms, while I felt damn near ostracized except for a select few family members who refused to fuck with him because of how he'd chosen to fuck over me.

If I had my way, he'd have been thrown from the roof of the building – onto a big bean bag or something that was put there last minute, but still. That was not, however, how that cookie crumbled.

Instead of settling for crumbs, I packed up my shit and did what I'd wanted to do for damn near a decade anyway.

I went to work with my cousins.

"I'm not even stressing it," I said, *although* I hadn't hung a single decoration in the apartment over the bar – Laken's old place that was mine now, since he'd purchased a condo with his wife. I hadn't even brought anything with me and had purposely avoided those areas in stores over the few weeks I'd been here.

Lark gave me a *look*, letting me know she damn well knew better than to believe the lie coming out of my mouth, but she just pursed her lips as she released the hug, clearly choosing not to address it.

Yet.

But I knew her enough to know it would come.

In the meantime, I went back to the same thing as before – slogging through those damn mistletoe mules. Eventually, the crowd started thinning out into the more "usual" crowd of first responders and hospital staff that *Night Shift* was a staple for.

Once the bar service was all caught up, I took the

opportunity to peek at my phone, immediately frowning at what I saw on the screen.

"Can we talk? – Rex."

"No the fuck we cannot," I answered aloud, but didn't actually respond to his inquiry. The only reason I hadn't full on blocked his ass was because our jobs at Kimble Bourbon were tangentially related enough that sometimes I *had* to communicate with him. But now that I'd moved on to take on a sales management role at Kimble *Brewing*, there wasn't shit he needed to say to me.

Thank *God* I didn't give his ass any babies.

I slipped the phone back in my pocket just as Lark approached again, this time with a tablet in hand, asking about the commemorative champagne glasses I'd insisted on for the New Year's festivities at the bar. It only fell into my purview because I thought it would be a cool item to add for merchandising – we could mark up all the champagne and champagne cocktail sales that night because they got to keep the glass.

"The delivery is set for Tuesday, but it'll probably be Wednesday honestly," I told her. "Thank goodness Keris got the design back to me on such a tight turnaround."

"I told you she could do it – that girl is a freaking gem," Lark gushed on her way to the back, making me grin. The way she'd embraced her sister-in-law was such a sharp contrast to the way she'd been about Rex, and with good reason I hadn't quite been able to see.

As a matter of fact, Laken – Lark's brother, Keris' husband, my cousin – hadn't been that much of a fan either. Nor had their other brother, Phoenix. Damn near everybody else in my family acted like Rex was the second coming of Jesus, which in retrospect, had probably influenced my rose-colored glasses where it came to him.

Hell, even now he was still getting "family" treatment, despite the ugliness he'd levied against me in the process of our divorce. My parents were still holding a grudge about my "lack of effort" where it came to fighting for our marriage.

But why the hell would I be fighting for someone who'd seen no issue with an ultra-public display of disrespect?

I'd rather eat a bourbon barrel.

Right on cue, my phone buzzed in my pocket again – him, again.

"Are you at the bar tonight? - Rex"

What bar?

This bar?

"I hope this motherfucker isn't stupid enough to show up here uninvited," I said – to myself again, not to him.

I was in the middle of my snap decision to simply block his ass when I got a reply — a verbal one — to my not-so-private fussing.

"I hope he ain't either chile."

My gaze jumped from my phone to the bar, where

a seat that had been empty a moment ago was now occupied by one of the most beautiful people I'd ever seen in real life. Sharply groomed brows, juicy coils of thick natural hair with impeccably faded sides, sculpted nose, chin, lips, and flawless butter-pecan skin that sparked a quick twinge of envy – the maintenance budget had to be insane for skin like that. His elbows were propped on the bar, and the fingers folded under his chin were full of gold and black rings in varying sizes and shapes – his ears held similar adornments.

And yet, with all the beauty and bling, his eyes – thick lashes framing fiery copper brown orbs – were what pulled my attention the most.

Still, I found my manners to take the few steps to approach with a smile. "My bad for the show – what can I get for you?"

"Your choice sweetheart – just don't knock me on m'ass too bad," he answered, his accent making me tip my head to the side.

"Where you from?" I couldn't help asking — a question that earned me a smile with a *lot* of mischief behind it.

"I'm from all over the place, bon ami."

My eyebrows bunched together. "Nah, I think you're from the gulf," I said, eyes narrowed as I examined him again. "Matter of fact... the more I look at you, I feel like you're one of my people."

"If you think so, then I am," he replied, the subtle rasp to his voice making me smile for a reason I couldn't place. His heavy accent turned *think* into something more like *thank* and it was... soothing, somehow. "You gone make me that drink, cher?"

"Fa 'sho," I told him with a grin, turning to grab ingredients. I cringed to myself when I realized I'd gotten ingredients for another damn mistletoe mule, but I went with it, remembering his plea to not get too faded. When I turned back, he was fingering a coin around his neck, but he dropped it as soon as I handed him the drink.

"What's a pretty thing like you doing letting some couyon stress you out?" he asked, swirling the metallic cup before he took a drink. "If you don't mind my asking..."

I probably should've, but I didn't – I looked him right in the eyes and answered. "I'm trying my best not to."

"You think so?"

My eyes went wide. "What makes you think I'm not?"

"The wretchedness behind your eyes."

I... maybe wasn't expecting such a direct answer?

My mouth dropped open in surprise, and I straightened a little. "Well damn," I laughed a bit, shaking my head. I... didn't know I looked so... *wretched.*"

"You're all twisted up," he shrugged, taking another sip from his drink. "You gon' have to get it together – unravel all those knots."

"What the hell are you talking about?"

The question was serious, but my tone was light – I wasn't bothered, just confused.

"I'm talking about the fact that ain't nobody gotta put no roots on you – you got your own gris-gris going on, and it's a damn shame."

For a moment, I just looked at him, then grabbed the dish towel to wipe down the prep area behind the bar. "You know – you remind me of my cousin," I told him. "He was always on the spooky shit too."

"Is that good or bad?"

"The spooky shit?"

"That I remind you of your cousin."

"Oh!" I took a deep breath as I pushed the damp towel along the stainless steel counter. "It's... a little of both, I guess. Phoe was one of my favorite people *ever,* but... he isn't with us anymore."

"You really believe that?"

My eyebrow shot up. "You're making we wonder – I wouldn't be surprised if his ass came back in an equally fabulous form. Phoenix... that you?" I asked, looking the man in his eyes – which were *scarily* similar to my cousin's.

He just smirked, raising the metallic cup to his lips again as I shook my head. The towel slipped from my hand because I wasn't actually looking – I bent to pick it up, then tossed it into the discard bin with the other towels needing a good wash.

When I turned around again, his gaze was fixed on

me, startlingly intense. Before I could really react, he'd reached across the bar, grabbing my wrist to turn my palm upward. "You know you can't keep burying what's meant to be above the ground, right? It's just gone keep comin' up."

I frowned. "You some kinda seer? I hope not, cause I *know* you're not talking about me entertaining my clown ex-husband."

"That ain't all the past you've got, cher."

My face wrinkled in confusion. "*Huh?*"

"It ain't that hard to understand."

"Bullshit."

He grinned. "You want your joie de vivre back, girly?"

"You sellin' it?"

"You ain't gotta buy it, but it's gone cost," he said, dipping his head a bit. "This ain't you, and you ain't been you, and you not gone *be* you until you take a good look at yourself."

"Okay Phoenix, I *know* this is you now."

He sat back a little, laughing, but didn't release my hand. "You ready to get back to yourself, bon ami?"

"How can I be your friend if I don't know you?" I countered with a smile.

"I'm a friend to many, marauder to some. You ready?"

Eyes narrowed, I tried to tell myself to pull my hand away, but for whatever reason... I couldn't. Instead, I offered the briefest nod – immediately, he brought up his other ring-filled hand, tracing a shape I couldn't follow with one long-nailed finger.

And then as quickly as it started, it was over – he released my hand and sat back, finishing the rest of his drink.

"What was that?" I asked, closing my hand into a fist.

Those copper orbs flashed with mischief yet again. "You'll see."

I shook my head. "You ain't slick," I said, turning to look around for Lark or Laken, needing someone else to see what I saw in this man. Just then, Lark came strolling from the back, and I flagged her down. "Tell me who he looks like," I pointed.

She looked up, following my finger, then looked back at me. "Who?"

"The guy right there," I said, turning to face where he was sitting. "He looks like..."

... nobody.

He was gone.

Only the cup was there, with a crisp twenty-dollar bill tucked underneath.

TWO

I SHOULD'VE ASKED HIS NAME.

That thought kept playing in my head as I waited for the last hour of my shift to tick by. *Bartender* wasn't my designated role in the company, but Laken liked for everybody to spend at least a bit of time either behind the bar, or the floor, or down in the brewery. I'd gotten a crash course on all three when I first arrived.

For the most part, I'd chosen the bar for my mandatory one shift a week, since it was where I could kinda... zone out.

Which I'd found myself doing unfortunately more and more often in the last year – so much existential crisis-ing. I hated it, because before, I was... *happy.*

Were you though?

I frowned at the thought.

Yes, of course I'd been happy.

I had a great career with room for growth at my family company, great friends, great house, great husband, great wardrobe.

Everything was... *great.*

Except... was it?

This ain't you, and you ain't been you, and you not gone be you until you take a good look at yourself.

Out of everything that gorgeous stranger said to me, *that* had stood out so much.

And the more I thought about it, the more I wondered if it was deeper than just not being myself because of the divorce.

Had I really been *myself* even before that?

"Kat..."

My head popped up from where I'd been doing a bit of multi-tasking myself – I was supposed to be soliciting new accounts to carry the various Night Shift brews, including Laken's precious ginger beer he'd been so amped about. In the lull, I'd been going over my list of potential bars and restaurants between here, the Heights, and Sugar Valley, which wasn't that far.

Now, my attention was taken by one of the last people I cared to see right now.

"Reginald... how can I help you?" I asked, putting my tablet down and folding my arms in front of me. "Need to know the nearest intersection you can step into, or...?"

"You don't have to be like that."

"I think I do."

I refused to give him the satisfaction of saying more, just staring at him until he shifted uncomfortably on his feet, then took a seat at the bar.

"I don't want a drink," he said, and I raised an eyebrow.

"Good, because I wasn't making you one. Again – how can I help you?"

"We need to talk."

"There is not a thing in the world I need to discuss with you."

"Fine – *I'll* talk then," he said. "I think... I think I made a mistake."

My eyes narrowed, face pulled into a scowl. "What the hell does that have to do with me?"

"You were the mistake."

"The feeling is mutual, motherfucker."

"No, I mean... shit," he groaned, scrubbing a hand over his mouth and chin. "I mean that... the divorce was a mistake. "From letting that even become an option in my mind, to the way I went about it, to actually seeing it through... it was all just... the worst possible misstep. Kat... I *miss you*."

He said that and then sat back, shoulders dropped as if he'd just released the weight of the world from then. His face remained focused though, unimpeded by my obvious frown.

Confident.

If I had to be honest... it was one thing I'd loved about him.

From the moment we met, that self-assurance had bordered on arrogance — he was *sure* I was going to be his wife. We were going to be a power couple, and we'd work our way up to the executive level at Kimble Bourbon, and have a big ass house full of kids.

It was exactly the life my mother wanted for me – the picture-perfect fantasy she implanted in me from as long as I could remember. It was so deeply rooted that, for the longest time, I thought I wanted it for myself.

I *did* want it for myself, and we were well on our way.

I was *happy*.

I loved being on his arm – he was tall and handsome, and *so* affectionate. He was good to me, and we had a good life, and then he just... flipped the script on me.

I *still* wondered what I'd missed.

What the hell had taken us from couple goals to him embarrassing me — *rejecting me* — in such a cruel manner?

The shit he pulled was downright *mean*, and I would never, ever forget it.

I'd never be over it.

"What do you expect me to say right now, Rex?" I asked, with genuine curiosity. "What is this? Exactly a year ago, you waited until I was literally *surrounded* by people to have me served with divorce papers. You ignored my calls, my texts, I went home and your shit was *gone*. With no explanation. And now you're, what... *sorry?*"

"Yes," he nodded, sitting forward like he'd just had some damn breakthrough.

I laughed, but nothing was funny. "You're damn right," I agreed. "Sorry. Pathetic. All of that – but I'm not," I explained. "If you think I would *ever* accept... what is this?"

He sighed. "It's... I guess an attempt at some reconci—"

"Don't even let the rest of that come out of your mouth," I said, eyes wide. "I'm asking this as seriously as possible – have you lost your mind?"

"I'm dead serious, Kat – this shit is... this is dumb. *I* was dumb," he quickly clarified. "I know what I want, and who I want that with, and we're both too old to start from scratch and still have that."

I scoffed. "So your proposal is that I forget you humiliated and divorced me—"

"I didn't *want* to divorce you," he interrupted, and my mouth dropped open.

"Excuse me? I have paperwork and a big ass lawyer bill that would disagree."

"It was never supposed to get there," he said. "Not... *there*. I thought I could... I don't know, shock you into seeing reason."

I uncrossed my arms to prop my hands at my waist, barely believing what I'd just heard. "So you...

disgraced me in front of all my peers, my family to...
manipulate me?"

"I... I know it was wrong," he quickly added. "And
I know it was idiotic, I just... I didn't know what else to
do, when you weren't *listening*."

"There was nothing for me to listen to," I hissed,
planting my hands on the bar as I leaned over it. "We
had a *plan*. A strategy that worked for both us – a
timeline that worked for both of us, and you just—"

"It *never* worked for me," he admitted. "I never
wanted that!"

"So you *lied*?"

"No, I made it work!" he challenged. "And I hoped
you would see the light. I was offering you every
woman's dream life, Kat."

"Every woman doesn't aspire to her husband's
black card and pretty chocolate babies as the epitome
of accomplishment, Rex! It's a beautiful life for some
women, but it is *not* a life for *me!* Just like you had
professional goals, and dreams, *so did I*," I whisper-
yelled, trying to keep some composure. "And you let
me believe we were a fucking team, while you were
plotting to strip that from me."

He sat back, letting out a deep sigh. "I said it was
wrong."

"Yeah – you realize after you've wasted damn near
a decade of my life!"

"It doesn't have to be a waste, we can—"

"*We* can't do a damn thing. Not now, or ever."

"Why not?"

That question... *stunned* me.

Not because I didn't have a quick, offensive answer – *because I hope your dick falls off next time you try to use it* — or even a more vulnerable one – *because you hurt me beyond repair and I love myself too much to allow you access to me again.*

But because the real, *for real* truth was that...

"I don't want that anymore," I said, straightening up. There was no malice in my tone, just the same certainty *he* usually had. "I'm not sure... I don't think it's what I ever *really* wanted."

"What isn't what you wanted?" he asked, confused.

"The whole... power couple thing. The big suburban house. The four kids, the dog, the stuffy corporate job," I muttered. "None of that shit was ever... *me*."

"Kat... that's nonsense."

"It's not," I shook my head. "What I want is... *this*," I gestured around me. "A hands-on job that actually makes a difference, where I actually enjoy working with my family. A cute condo with no yard upkeep. Two inches of hair that doesn't have to be perfectly silk-pressed every time I step outside," I said, running a hand through the ruthless haircut I'd gotten damn near as soon as I got to town.

Thank God my mother hadn't seen it yet, cause it would be a *problem*.

"I think you just needed some time away from it all. A break – of course a different lifestyle appeals to you right now, but in two months?" he argued, and I shook my head.

"You don't get it, Rex – *this* is what I've fantasized about. When I wasn't pretending to be perfectly happy and content with what we had."

"So, suddenly you had a terrible life?"

I scoffed. "No, it was a great life... it just wasn't mine."

Rex pushed out another of those disappointed sighs that were *quickly* getting real tired. "Listen... How about after the New Year, you come back to—"

"You're not listening."

"No, *you* aren't listening," he fussed. "This is done, Katari," he demanded, with a little bass in his voice – the kind that used to have me damn near purring, but now it was just grating. "We had our fuckup, mistakes were made on both sides, and now it's *done*. You wrap things up here so you leave Laken in a bind, and then you—"

"I'm seeing somebody," I interrupted, knowing those words would stop his bullshit in its' tracks.

His head tipped into a slant. "What did you say?"

"I said... I'm seeing somebody," I repeated. "I'm *fucking* somebody."

He recoiled like he'd been slapped. "You've barely been here a month, how—"

"I guess I'm a hot commodity, and there's all these buff firefighters, and—"

"That's enough," he snapped, face pulled into a scowl. "I don't understand how you could... *why* you would..."

"You don't understand why a single woman would be involved with someone?"

"You're not a single woman, you're my *wife*."

"*Was* your wife," I corrected. "And now... I'm just Katari. *Happily*."

He stared at me a moment, then his face pulled into a sneer. "You know what... fine. *Fuck you*," he growled, pushing back from the bar to stand up. "I can't believe I came here feeling bad for your ungrateful ass."

All I could do was grin at his sudden switch up.

Somehow... it wasn't remotely a surprise.

"I hope you find what you're looking for," was all I said before he turned in a huff to storm out, taking the extra effort to slam the door behind him.

Once he was gone, I glanced at the time.

Yes.

Time to clock out.

THREE

Three

This ain't you, and you ain't been you, and you not gone be you until you take a good look at yourself.

That shit kept me up half the night.

Instead of giving in to the desire to simply drown in my thoughts though, I muted them by getting a bit of work done – sending off an email to all the prospective bars and restaurants I wanted to talk to about Night Shift.

Would they respond to, or likely even *see* these emails from two in the morning on Christmas?

Of course not.

But when I popped up unannounced and in person next week, it would be something I could refer to. Even if I didn't get to talk to the person in charge of their spirit sales, it would bring the email to the front of their mind, and instead of either correspondence being a single contact, I'd already loaded *two*.

Third time was usually the charm.

It was a strategy that had worked countless times before, one I'd actually used for training at Kimble Bourbon. I had no problem employing it now because I was the one who'd developed it. One of the major keys was to not send a generic email – it needed to be specific to the personality and vibe of the establishment.

Which took a little time and research.

Neither one was a problem for me, especially since it wasn't a deep dive – that was reserved for cutting through reticence and competition. I'd already challenged myself that within six months, I'd have every single place on Lark's list serving at least two SKUs from *Night Shift*.

If nothing else, no one could *ever* say Katari Kimble didn't dominate a job role.

Exhaustion swept me off to dreamland with both my snacks and laptop still in the bed – when I woke up, it was because my phone was going off. Despite the early hour, I was quick to snatch it from the nightstand before I missed the call.

It was barely up to my ear, *hello* not even out of my mouth yet before I heard the Christmas song being crooned over the phone by my brother and his kids. I listened with a smile, genuinely glad he'd called, and more than happy to let the words, *"Merry Christmas y'all,"* leave my mouth when they were finally done.

I might do *some* complaining about my particular branch of the Kimble family tree, but never was I *ever* talking about Jaylin or Irina, my siblings. They were both older than me, and always had my back when it counted – they'd even been supportive of the move, knowing how being in Kentucky had been draining me.

Between the two of them, I burned an hour catching up with not just them but my nieces and nephews, listening to them chatter all about what they'd gotten for Christmas, how they were doing in school, all that stuff I loved.

And *did* eventually want for myself.

Despite what a few select people would have me believing, I had time. I was only a few months into my thirty-second year, and if you listened to Rex – or so much worse, *my mother* — you'd think my uterus was literally crumbling from my body, leaving behind a trail of dust. They both despised my unwillingness to let them move me on the topic.

I had a timeline, and every intention of sticking to it.

If things changed, they changed, but my *plan* would not.

It was the only way I was holding on to any semblance of control.

Although... I realized now just how effectively I'd been convinced that the marriage, career, kids, house in the suburbs thing was *my* plan.

When really...

This ain't you, and you ain't been you, and you not gone be you until you take a good look at yourself.

Before I graduated with the business degree, before I was supposed to work at the family company, *what had been the dream?*

Had there ever been a dream that was *just* mine?

Hell, since high school, and maybe even before that, my parents had built in certain expectations of me and my siblings — expectations Irina and Jaylen had lived up to. They were professionally successful, married, kids, the whole nine. And with an age gap of five years between each of us, leaving me as the baby, by the time I was even old enough to conceptualize adulthood and plans for it... there were already examples in place for me to follow.

So... I did.

And to what end, now?

I nearly jumped out of my skin at the chime of my phone, catching me off guard.

Mother Dearest.

For a moment, I toyed with the idea of not answering, but it was Christmas.

I *had* to answer.

I didn't have to offer any flavor though.

Because of that, the conversation was stiff and

brief, and still not over soon enough. I hated being that way, but I had a hard time accepting any fault for the way things had ended up.

Why *should* I give any warmth and color to people who'd sided with my ex-husband?

It was fucked up.

Really fucked up.

The people I should've been able to depend on to surround me love and support had instead taken the position that I should meet Rex's demands – demands that directly contradicted the things we'd agreed to and explicitly outlined *before* signing a marriage certificate.

Of course, I knew now that it was a sham.

But because they agreed with him – because of their own selfish wants for *my* life... I was the one in the wrong for not bending or compromising, even though it was *all* a compromise.

Because again... that plan was never really, *truly* mine.

Another sound from my phone got my attention, but it was an email this time, instead of a call. My eyes went wide as I realized it was a reply to one of my early morning solicitations.

Ms. Kimble, thank you for reaching out!

Our owner is actually the one who facilitates our spirit sales, and he will not be back in office until mid-January. If by some chance you're available today, he has about a twenty-minute window in his schedule before our Christmas Brunch reservations come in. I understand that it's the holiday, so please don't feel obligated, but if you want to catch him before next month, this would be your chance. Otherwise, I can put you on his schedule for when he returns. Please let me know by ten this morning if you'd like to speak to him today.

- *Malonie Ford, Executive Assistant, Ascension*

My eyes shot up to where the time was displayed across the top of the screen.

9:38.

Shit.

The email had actually been in my box for nearly an hour, but between my musings and phone calls with family, it must've slipped by me.

I was already out of bed and on my feet, typing out a response while I rushed to the bathroom to get myself together. It wasn't a complete surprise they were open – *Night Shift* would be open later as well – so I'd already had the forethought to pick an outfit, even if I thought I wouldn't actually have occasion to put it on.

I *definitely* wanted to speak to him before mid-January.

I wanted that ball rolling as soon as possible.

I got myself presentable in twenty minutes flat, enough time to meet the rideshare that was going to take me a few blocks over to where Ascension was. I could have walked in a fairly short time, but the frigid temperatures and icy sidewalks eliminated the possibility from my mind. The last thing I needed was to be flustered from the cold, or worse — to bust my ass trying to get there.

I didn't know as much as I would've liked about Ascension, and didn't have time to look it up while going back and forth via text with my cousins to explain why I was going to be a little later than expected for the hangout we'd planned. By the time the car pulled up in front of the restaurant, barely five minutes after I'd gotten into it, I had an unexpected pit in my stomach.

A bit of nerves, yes, but also... *excitement.*

This was the kind of thing I'd wanted to be doing for Kimble Bourbon – *not* dealing with a bunch of stuffy corporate bullshit. Growing up, I'd always thought the alcohol sales reps were *so cool.* They didn't have to wear suits and stockings and all that. They got to meet potential clients where they were, clubbing and handing out shots. They got to travel. It looked *amazing.*

Then my mother explained that being a *"glorified bottle girl"* was absolutely not for me.

Now, I knew the job wasn't all glitz and glamor like I thought back then, but even with the "cons" the idea of it still interested me. I wouldn't exactly be jet setting anytime soon with Night Shift, but even *this* was a marked improvement – getting to go out and meet new people, working on my pitch in real time.

I was geeked.

Stepping into Ascension off the street was a feast for the senses. You walked into tasteful gray-blue décor that fit into a kind of aerial-esque feeling, like you were up in the sky. The aroma of the brunch menu hit hard, making my stomach twist in a knot to remind me of the breakfast I'd skipped.

The woman at the hostess stand had her head down, fingers flying over the keyboard in front of her as her head bobbed to the music, braids swaying along. Her eyes drifted up to me as I approached, and she offered a smile.

"Katari Kimble?" she asked, and I nodded confirmation. "Perfect – have a seat at the bar."

She gestured around a corner to where the actual restaurant opened up – a sea of booths and tables all trimmed in gold. Servers were all over the place, laughing and talking amongst themselves as they put the last touches on the place before it opened for brunch.

I took that seat at the bar out of the way, admiring the smooth, sky-like blue and white epoxy finish. It was the same surface as all the tables, continuing the theme in a way that was *just* shy of being campy. Whoever designed it had struck a pretty perfect balance.

While I waited, I thought through my still-in-development pitch in my head – the local popularity of

Night Shift, the origin story, the quality ingredients and care that went into each brew, the importance of buy-in from *other* established Black businesses to cement their status, the direct-from-distributor wholesale discounts we could offer – on, and on, and on.

As I sat there, I raked my nails across my right palm, trying to soothe a sudden itch I couldn't attribute to anything except nerves. Unbidden, I found myself tracing the shape the man at the bar had drawn, but all I could remember was the initial circle.

Then the air behind me shifted.

I turned in my seat, and immediately my eyes were drawn to a man, ambling into the main area of the restaurant from the back, where the offices had to be. His confident, casual stride faltered a bit when our gazes met, and a slow, sexy smirk spread across his lips.

There's no way.

FOUR

There's no way.

Except... there was definitely a way, and I could not *look* away.

Like my pupils were freaking magnetized to his, I maintained eye contact as he drew closer.

Smile or something, girl, damn!

As soon as I started to, he looked away, distracted by the approach of a staff member with a question.

Thank God.

His diversion was a necessary reprieve from whatever the hell looking right into his eyes was making me feel. Still, I couldn't help glancing back in his direction, mind racing as I processed what was happening.

After all these years, why does he look this good?

He was dressed in all black – black sweater, black

jeans, black and white sneakers, gold chain. A combo that by definition was casual, but the drape of the fabrics, the crispiness of the white and deep saturation of blacks said... luxury.

This was a very different man than the one I met a decade ago.

When it was clear his conversation was wrapping up, I looked away so I wouldn't be caught staring at him.

As if it mattered.

"To say I'm surprised would be an understatement."

Shit.

I'd been so busy trying not to pay him too much attention I'd allowed him to sneak up on me, making his opening statement from much closer than he should probably be. I turned on my stool now to face him, trying to guess what might be happening in his head.

Futile.

Unlike his initial smirk, his expression now was inscrutable – and he was patient, apparently, not offering me any more words.

The proverbial ball was in my court.

"Surprised in a good way, or...?"

His face softened a little. "Let's call it neutral until you've said your piece."

"Sure," I nodded, gesturing for him to take a seat.

I expected him to leave a few seats between us – a

respectable distance. Instead, he perched himself right next to me, then turned, legs open, with one foot perched on *my* footrest.

"So... this isn't a personal visit," he said, his eyes roving my face, clearly drinking me in.

Calculating all the ways *I'd* changed.

"It's not," I admitted. "I'm here representing *Night Shift* – a very popular, Black-owned local microbrewery and bar that recently started bottling some signature brews."

"I'm very familiar with *Night Shift*." He said, his emotion still indecipherable in his tone.

I nodded. "Of course. But, we want the *world* to know about *Night Shift*, so we're looking at expansion opportunities."

Derrick tipped his head. "This is the same company that makes *Kimble Bourbon*, right?"

"Not the same company, but the same family, yes. The founder, Laken Kimble, branched off because he wanted to do something new that the family didn't support. But, with no short supply of determination and drive, he built it anyway. We would love if you'd consider offering a few of our brews in your bar inventory."

I was sure I sounded like some corporate shill, regurgitating practiced talking points.

Because I *was*.

I'd hoped for a more organic conversation, but I

absolutely hadn't expected to be speaking with Derrick Allen.

The years had been kind.

Very kind.

Back then, he'd been clean-shaven and perfectly faded, with a "pretty boy" appeal I hadn't been able to resist. There was nothing "boyish" about him now – he'd dropped the razors *and* the clippers in favor of the kind of lush, thick coils you just wanted to sink your fingers in.

Really though, it was his eyes for me, reminiscent of perfectly steeped sun tea – one of my favorite things. I couldn't say with any certainty that it factored into how I'd felt about him that summer, but I couldn't say the opposite either.

They were still the same – that perfect translucent brown, sparkling with interest and a near perpetual impression that he was on the verge of laughing at *something*.

I was glad that hadn't changed.

He had certainly changed though, and not just physically – the young man I knew back then... he wasn't... *lost* per se, but he definitely didn't have any kind of solid footing, or goals, or... plans.

It had been a sticking point for me, honestly.

When we met... the month I spent in Blackwood had been fun, but it wasn't *for* fun – I was being groomed for my place in the family conglomerate. So while a summer spent in the company of a handsome, well-endowed near-stranger was inarguably a good time, it could not be a *long* one.

Something that had been hard enough to verbalize, and I *knew* it couldn't have been easy to hear.

"I've already considered it," he said, in a tone that didn't *exactly* suggest a favorable answer. "I've been considering it since my assistant told me about your email."

I raised an eyebrow. "And?"

He didn't reply – he turned away, looking toward the bar.

I didn't want to say the wrong thing, so instead I said nothing, following his gaze to the bottles lined up row by row. All the way to the top shelf.

Holding several bottles of *Kimble Bourbon*.

"Should I take that to mean you're not holding a grudge?" I asked, unable to help myself.

He didn't pretend not to know what I was talking about, but all the same, his response was, "What makes you I would?"

"Maybe... the way we parted?"

He leaned in, meeting my gaze. "You mean when you hurt my damn feelings?" he asked, then quickly looked around to ensure no one had overheard his confession, making me smile.

"I'm sorry," I said. "That wasn't my intention – you know that, right?"

He tipped his chin. "I do. That doesn't change the

fact that you ruined me for all other women, though,"
he teased, and I laughed.

"I think you're giving me too much credit, Derrick.
It was a *month*."

"It was a good ass month," he countered. "Maybe
better for me than you?"

I frowned. "What makes you say *that*?"

"Because you seem to have made more of a lasting
impression on me than I made on you. You moved on,
got married. I got... a reputation among my friends as
the whore of the group," he laughed, and I did
too, but...

"How did you know I got married?" I asked, and he
gestured at my hand.

"That little permanent dent on your finger," he
answered. "What's his name?"

"Let's not go there."

"Damn, I can't know my competition's name?"

My eyes went wide. "Competition?!"

"I said what I said," he countered, with a cocky grin
that... *shit*.

*What **is** that man's name?*

"You know, you never *really* answered me about
stocking *Night Shift* here," I said, trying to change the
subject, which made him chuckle.

"I'll have a purchase order sent over by tomorrow."

"*Really?*" I asked, grinning.

"Yeah. Anything for *that* smile," he said, reaching
out for a short caress of my chin.

Whew, shit.

Time to go.

"I'll make sure you get a great discount on that first order," I said, slipping off my barstool.

He was right there with me too, his stocky frame engulfing mine in a hug that was riiiight on the line of too much.

He didn't cross it though.

"It was good to see you, Katari," he said, muttering the words into my hair before pressing a quick kiss on my forehead.

"Likewise," I whispered back, then promptly cleared my throat. "I... guess I'll see you around," I said.

"You will."

It was a mistake, wearing heels.

I couldn't scurry my ass out of there like I wanted unless I wanted to end up twisting an ankle, so I kept it as cute as I could. And just before I made it out unscathed, he called my name, forcing me to look back.

"Have dinner with me tonight."

Not a request.

A statement.

Shit.

There was no harm in considering it, in weighing the invitation.

But before I could do so, my mouth was already moving, with — seemingly — no assistance from my brain.

"Yes."

FIVE

Y*ES*.

Yes?

Who the hell agreed to Christmas dinner with an old flame while her current – potential – flame was alone on Christmas?

Me, apparently.

I hadn't been bluffing Rex when I told him I was seeing – fucking – somebody. I had, maybe a little, fudged the seriousness of it.

There was a reason Marley didn't even cross my mind until *after* I'd exchanged numbers with Derrick to meet up tonight, after our planned time with friends and family.

It wasn't *that* deep.

We'd met randomly my *first* night in town. I was still so emotionally raw from my semi-spontaneous move that I'd welcomed the influx from the Thanksgiving visitor crowd, losing myself in the making of drinks.

His card declined.

A big, waving red flag anyone could see from a mile away.

But he was fine – *real fine* – and he had cash to cover his tab. I didn't need or want somebody to help with bills, and I for damn sure wasn't looking to *build*. Luckily, what I thought I needed was exactly what he offered – dick, which he delivered in skilled abundance.

He was nice to talk to, as well.

He knew a lot about a lot, so pillow talk actually held a lowkey appeal.

I... liked him.

I didn't want to marry him, move in with him, none of that, but I'd be lying if I claimed that what was borne of lust and escapism hadn't cultivated an interest in... possibilities.

He was Rex's polar opposite, which had been refreshing over these last few weeks. Marley was an artist – the stereotypical damn near starving kind. He was young – grown, but too young to take seriously. His place was always a mess, he'd been talking about getting a haircut since we met, and he never, *ever* knew exactly what day of the week it was.

He never talked about the stock market because he didn't fucking care.

The idea of making plans for his future was an assault to his nature.

His art was a point of expression, not a source of income – I had no clue what the man did for income.

The chaos was endearing.

Or... distracting.

Maybe both.

Whatever it was, the *indisputable* fact was that I enjoyed him – enough that there was a wrapped Christmas gift waiting for him in my closet at home.

A not-remotely-cheap one.

Even more reason he should've crossed my mind before agreeing to dinner with a man who'd made a mess of my panties with just a *hug*.

Back at my place, I grabbed his gift and headed right back out – I already knew he was home. He preferred not to make a big deal of "commercial holidays", but he wasn't opposed enough that a gift would be offensive.

And... admittedly... if I fucked *him* today, I wasn't scandalous enough to also fuck Derrick tonight. It was a shaky plan, but the only one I had.

When I got to the door of his apartment, I could already hear music floating from inside. For a moment, I hesitated to knock, reluctant to interrupt him if he was painting.

Then something that sounded suspiciously like a gunshot went off outside, and I got over my reluctance.

Quickly.

I started up a pretty firm, pretty *constant* knock, making sure I was loud enough to be heard over his music without sounding like I was the police. It wasn't out of the ordinary for me to show up without any correspondence, but it had never been an issue before, so I had no reason to suspect it might be one now.

An assumption that was, shortly, proven wrong.

He opened the door looking wild as ever – hair mashed in like he'd just left the bed, out of breath, wearing... nothing.

Not even boxers.

His dick was hard.

And... wet.

As was his face.

"Oh."

That was... literally all I could say to the man standing in front of me, unabashedly covered in another woman's pussy fluids.

"*Kat*," he greeted, soooo casual.

So casual.

"You wanna come in?" he gestured vaguely inside. "You can meet Pilar – she'd *love* you."

"*Oh*," I breathed, confused, but also... not at all confused. "I... no. No, thank you."

"You sure? She's an ass woman, and you... well..." he smirked, *conspiratorially*, like he was offering me the time of my life.

And... shit, maybe he was.

But also...

"No, I'm sure," I said, lifting my arm to hand him the bag I'd slid his wrapped gift into. "Merry Christmas."

His eyes went wide, mouth spreading into a grin like a kid. "Seriously? Thank you, you didn't have to do this."

"I know," I nodded. "But... you enjoy, okay?"

"You sure you don't want to come in? She can just watch – she likes that too."

"I've never been more sure of anything," I called over my shoulder as I walked away, because...

What the fuck?

I... wasn't even mad.

What would be the point?

There hadn't been a conversation about monogamy because I hadn't been *thinking* about monogamy, which was probably idiotic.

It was *clearly* idiotic, because *clearly* it was quite the casual thing for him. While for me it had been...

What, bitch? What exactly had it been?

... different.

Just... different, which had been what I thought I needed, but the feeling I was left with now had me wondering about the accuracy of that.

Seriously.

It was one thing to get immersed in a fling that was *purely* for the fun of it, and remaining grounded in that. It was something else entirely to think about... what had I called it?

Possibilities.

Just because he was such a sharp contrast to my ex-husband.

I didn't even have to wonder what I'd been doing, because I could see it so clearly. There was some void I was trying to fill by jumping from one situation that wasn't what I wanted to one that was a direct contradiction of it all.

And *it* wasn't what I wanted either.

This ain't you, and you ain't been you, and you not gone be you until you take a good look at yourself.

Shit.

I hated, like *really hated* the accuracy of the first part.

This shit with Marley absolutely wasn't me, and the shit with Rex hadn't been me either. I couldn't live a life based on what had been decided for me, and I couldn't live one purely based on rebellion to it, either.

At some point... I was going to have to figure out what the hell really worked for *me*.

———

"SHOES, KAT?! SHOES!?" LARK TURNED AWAY FROM me to look at Keris, seeking backup for her exasperation.

Keris shrugged. "What's wrong with buying a man shoes?" she asked, then took a swig from her drink and Lark's eyes bugged even wider.

"*Pauve ti bete*," she groused, shaking her head. "I can excuse her not knowing," she gestured at Keris, but *you*," – she jabbed a finger in my shoulder — "Oughta be *shamed*."

"Don't do the faux Cajun shit with me," I laughed.

"Nothing *faux* about it, cher."

Oh, she was *definitely* playing it up – she had an accent, like most Kimbles, but she was putting more than a little extra twang on, and sprinkling in... *lagniappe*.

"I feel like it's got something to do with giving him something he can use to run away," Keris mused, and Lark nodded.

"That's what they say – give a man shoes, he'll walk right out of your life."

"Good to know – let me make a mental note – don't buy Laken any shoes."

I sucked my teeth. "His ass ain't going nowhere anyway," I assured.

"Definitely not," Lark agreed, then leaned into her sister-in-law. "But just in case..."

"Y'all are a mess," I chuckled, picking up my glass – a night shift pint glass I was using for a *very* over-poured cocktail.

"Says the woman who got invited to an impromptu Christmas threesome..." Lark teased. "When he said the girl liked ass... do you think that meant they were gonna double-penetrate you? Her with a strap..."

I bit my lip, really considering it. "You know... it doesn't sound terrible, does it?"

"What doesn't sound terrible?" Laken asked, stopping at the booth where we were gathered.

"Nothing," I said, but Lark had already started talking.

"Kat almost got spit-roasted by her sneaky-link and *his* sneaky link."

Laken's mouth dropped open for just a moment, then he laughed. "I mean... shout out to you really living it up?" he said, grabbing Keris by the hand to take her with him as he left.

"I'm having the *hardest* time remembering why the hell I've been calling y'all my favorite cousins," I countered to his back, shaking my head. "Be nicer to me, it's Christmas."

Lark fake gasped. "I'm always nice to you!"

"So nice you didn't tell me I'd be running into Derrick when I told y'all I was going to Ascension this morning?"

Her eyebrows shot up. "Derrick Allen? Why would I have warned you about..." her eyes narrowed. "Wait... What's the story there?"

"There isn't—"

"Don't lie."

I blew out a sigh, flopping back in the booth. "*Fine.* Remember when I came up here with Laken like ten years ago, trying to get Kimble Bourbon in more places than just the south?"

It was right before he split off to do his own thing – probably the reason he'd chosen Blackwood.

She gave me a slow nod. "I do…"

"Well…"

Lark's lips parted in surprise as she looked back at the screen. "Are you telling me what I think you're telling me?"

"That depends on what you think I'm telling you…"

She turned back to me with a smirk. "I think you're telling me that Derrick Allen's refusal to stock Night Shift at the bar in Ascension is actually *not* because of some supposed exclusivity discount he gets from a competitor?"

"Wait, *what?*" I asked, eyes wide. "What are you talking about?"

"When his restaurant first opened, five or six years ago, Laken and I sat down with him, and he *flatly* refused to put Night Shift in his bar," Lark explained. "At the time, he claimed it was because he had some sort of hookup that would only stay in place if he only stocked from that brewery. He was perfectly cordial, so we never had a reason to think it was anything other than what he said. But now I'm wondering… was it *actually* because my gorgeous baby cousin broke his heart?"

"I did *not* break that man's heart," I denied – a little too firmly, based on the look that spread across Lark's face.

"You don't even look like *you* believe that, so *I* definitely don't," she laughed. "What the hell happened? Y'all were only up here for what, a month? Or did you and Derrick have a little long-distance thing going after you went back to school?"

"I *wouldn't* do long-distance – that was part of the problem," I admitted. "It was good – a little *too* good while it lasted, but... it wasn't meant to be more than it was. Not that I could tell."

Lark raised an eyebrow at me. "Meaning...?"

"He wasn't... giving... *husband* vibes."

When I said that, Lark gave a deep, knowing nod.

We weren't that far apart in age, and had a lot in common – including mothers who were relentless with the *get married, have my grandbabies, keep your house perfect like I did* pressure.

Unlike me, Lark hadn't folded.

"So... what happened?" she asked. "I mean, he clearly hates you, so I'm assuming it was a no."

"He doesn't hate me!" I exclaimed, eyes wide. "I mean... he *did* have Kimble Bourbon stocked now..."

"Oh, in that case... clearly that man is in love with you still."

"Lark, *please*," I laughed. "How did we go from clear hate to clear love that fast?"

"I'm just telling it as I see it," she shrugged. "No, seriously though... what happened?"

"Nothing happened. He said he was sending a purchase order, and then... he asked me to dinner.

Tonight. And I said yes. Which I felt bad about, which was why I showed up at Marley's—"

"And almost got double-fucked," Lark said, making me break into a peal of laughter.

"Why are you so obsessed with that?" I asked, and she reached across the tabletop to grab my hands.

"I was living through you, Kat – one of us should get the most freaky shit imaginable done to her, and if it's not going to be me, well..."

"Wait, why can't it be you? I thought you were seeing somebody?"

She sighed, sitting back. "It's a somebody I'm not supposed to be seeing, so I'm trying to... be blind," she huffed. "I think you should go back over there."

"I'm *not* going back over there," I laughed. "I... am going to go upstairs, and get ready for dinner with Derrick, I guess."

"Where are y'all going?"

"He wants me to come back to the restaurant. To cook for me."

"Oooh," Lark gushed. "Can he cook?"

"I have no idea," I shrugged. "When we met, he didn't have any... ambition, I guess. Well, no, that's not quite it. He didn't know what he wanted to do with his life to get after it, you know? And I was *so certain*. Or I thought I was."

Lark sighed. "We had the same indoctrination, babe. You know I get it."

"Yeah, but... you and Laken, and even Phoenix, in a lot of ways... y'all split."

"At risk of damn near being excommunicated," she reminded me. "Some of the family *still* doesn't fuck with us. And my momma is *still* mad about my naked ring finger and empty womb."

"I know, but... *shit*," I breathed, glaring at my empty glass. "Now... I'm here, you know? And where the hell do I go from here?"

Lark smiled. "You... go to dinner."

SIX

So... I went to dinner.

As strange as it was to thrust myself into something so far removed from the way I would normally spend Christmas, somehow it just felt... *fitting*.

Keris and Lark had insisted that I aim at full-blown sexy instead of just showing up in my sweaterdress from earlier – a suggestion I quickly decided was the right choice.

The sound Derrick made when he helped me out of my coat was all the answer I needed.

"You know this don't make no damn sense, right?" he asked, stepping back to get a good look. "You weren't supposed to get finer."

I raised an eyebrow. "Why not?"

"Cause you broke my heart – how can I get my misogynistic revenge on you now?"

"Oh, is that what this is?" I laughed as he dropped my coat off at the area behind the hostess stand, then led me on into the restaurant. When he let me know to meet him at Ascension, I hadn't realized it would actually be closed, and we'd be the only people inside.

"Not at all," he assured. "I'm fucking around, but... *seriously,* Kat... I'm glad to see you looking good. *Doing good.*"

"Thank you – the feeling is mutual," I told him as I accepted the seat he offered at a booth tucked away near the back. "I'm not sure why I wasn't expecting to see you again."

"Because many people with pie in the sky plans don't ever actually see them through – what you thought was going to happen with me," he said as he took the seat across from me.

I sighed. "Derrick, it wasn't that I thought you wouldn't do anything with your life. I just... I needed somebody who knew what *that thing* was," I explained. "Or... I *thought* I needed that, at least."

"I won't front like it didn't hurt," he said as he picked up the bottle of wine already waiting on the table, uncorking it before pouring us both glasses. "But... I also won't pretend not to understand. Honestly... when I see my servers and hostesses have these men around here grinning in their face, I'm *quick* to tell them "potential doesn't pay bills"," he chuckled.

My mouth dropped. "Now, isn't that a little hypocritical?!"

"Maybe," he shrugged. "But like I said... many people will sell you a dream that never amounts to anything and stifle *you* in the process. I don't want to see that happen to these young ladies... with hindsight, of course."

"Of course," I chuckled. "Cause you were *not* thrilled with me when it happened."

"I sure as hell wasn't," he laughed. "But you know what? I was determined to prove you wrong, and now... here we are." He grabbed his glass, tipping it in my direction.

I nodded, finally picking up my wine glass – to accept his toast, and take a sip. "Here we are. A restaurant – I would *not* have expected that from you, I don't think."

"Well, it wasn't *the dream* at the time," he said. "I just knew I was going to do *something*. This was actually something my mother talked about doing a lot – she's the reason for the sky theme. She *loved* a good theme," he said, with a quiet, melancholy sort of chuckle.

"... *loved?*"

"She passed about a year after we met," he said. "Right as she was finally gathering up the courage to seek a small business loan. I committed myself to seeing her dream through – put every dime of the insurance policy she left into it. I was doing it for her, so failure wasn't an option."

"I thought you said you were trying to prove me

wrong."

"That too," he teased, shaking his head. "Nah, seriously though – it was all excellent motivation, you know? Now I have this place, and I just opened a lounge over in the Heights."

"Really?" I grinned. "Derrick, that's *amazing*. I'm really proud of you," I told him, *genuinely*.

Back when we first met, his big personality – and dick – had been a serious factor in what made him so attractive to me. He was always talking about wanting to do something with a big impact, wanting to have the kind of money that could grant any desire, stuff like that.

But it was... shallow, for lack of better phrasing.

He wanted those things, but had no idea how to get after them, and no desire to "waste away in a regular job". Which, I understood not wanting to do things you weren't passionate about, but by the same token...there was entirely too much pressure on *me* to have a certain life that I couldn't risk giving up my *own* potential.

Except... that still ended up being the sacrifice I was expected to make.

So what, ultimately, had I even gained?

"Tell me what's been up with you," Derrick said, pulling me from my internal musing. "I wanna know why you're not wearing that ring."

My eyes went wide. "Wow. I can't even have the dinner you promised first?"

"It's coming," he chuckled. "Don't deflect."

"But I enjoy deflecting."

"*Katari.*"

"I'm divorced," I admitted. "He served the papers at a company Christmas party."

Derrick's eyebrows shot up. "Damn. That's... *damn.*"

"Yeah. My sentiments exactly."

"He divorced *you?*"

I nodded. "Before we got married, we had a plan on when we'd have kids, we agreed on who would take time off, hiring nannies, the whole nine. But then, once we *got* married... he switched up. Not right off the bat, but some years in... he started trying to pressure me to quit my job, get off birth control, all this stuff that wasn't the agreement, *way* before what we'd planned for that. And when I didn't fold, he filed. Now he's saying it was never supposed to go that far."

"Oh shit – he was trying to bluff you?!"

"Apparently so," I chuckled. "But I'm not... I don't know. I'm just not that girl anymore. At first I was so caught in what things were *supposed* to be, according to my family, and now I'm just... over it. I called his bluff, and we went through the divorce despite him trying to drag it out. I quit my job at Kimble, and came to be with my cousins. It's really bittersweet, honestly, but now... it finally *feels* like how it's supposed to be. It feels like I'm settling into... *me.*"

This ain't you, and you ain't been you, and you not gone be you until you take a good look at yourself.

Unbidden, the strangers' words played in my head again, pulling a little smile to my face.

"Well...if I ever run into the man, I'm telling him thank you," Derrick said. "His loss was my gain."

I raised an eyebrow. "How you figure *that*?"

"I got my baby back," he said, giving me a look like it should've been obvious. "This is *fate*, girl."

"Fate? Seriously?" I laughed as his phone went off. I took another sip from my glass as he checked it, then gestured for me to wait a moment as he stood to go off toward the front of the restaurant.

While he was gone, I looked around – *Ascension* was all packed up for the night – chairs tucked away, all the tables wiped clean. It didn't occur to me until then that there weren't any sounds from the kitchen either, so how...

"*Dinner is served.*"

When I looked up, Derrick was headed back to me, with a bag of takeout in his hands.

"*Really?*" I giggled. "You invited me to *your* restaurant to eat somebody else's food?"

"I considered that," he said, "but in my defense..." he turned the bag so I could see the logo. "I thought nostalgia might make actually make the best impression."

He... wasn't wrong.

I actually had to swallow a bit of emotion at the sight of the *Battered Birds* logo – the same little spot we'd frequented *so* often during that fateful summer.

"You know... this reminds me – how are your friends?" I asked. "Kyle and Rob, right?"

"They're good – great, actually," Derrick said as he took his seat again. "Both married, actually. Rob married a woman named Iris, had a couple of kids. He's a principal now. Kyle left the league, started a business, got married. Him and Brandi actually *just* had a baby. A little girl. First girl for both of them."

"That's amazing, good for them," I mused. "And... what about you?" I asked, trying to keep my tone as casual as possible as I helped unpack the food – wings and fries and waffle sticks and Styrofoam cups of greens and macaroni. "Did you ever get married, have kids?"

"Nah," he admitted. "I was waiting for somebody."

"Stop it."

"No, for real," he insisted. "I'm not saying that I consciously *knew* that's what I was doing, but as I got older, I had to really look at the shit I was doing and wonder... was I *purposely* seeking temporary situations so I could be available when someone permanent came along?"

"Were you?"

He shrugged. "I can't call it. I just know that whenever I thought about it, about someone *permanent*... the only person who ever came to mind... was you."

"Wow. This is platinum level caking," I laughed, and he shook his head.

"Is it caking if I'm just telling you my truth?"

I bit down on my lip, chewing at it a bit before I shrugged. "I... I don't know," I told him. "And I don't mean to... I guess downplay your feelings. It's just... I feel very... uncomfortable."

"I'm making you feel uncomfortable?"

"Yes," I nodded. "But not in a bad way. I'm just processing."

"What are you processing?"

"The realization that I hadn't really been myself for a long time. And now that I'm back in Blackwood, now that... I've run into you. It's just... all these feelings, memories, that were faded and gray, and buried under the heaviness of this person I was "supposed" to be... it's all rushing back. Like *I'm* rushing back. Getting back my color, like the old folks say."

"I have never heard a Black person say that shit in my whole life," Derrick laughed, and... I laughed too, and it just felt so damn... *vibrant.*

All of it.

Eating the same food we used to eat, and talking like we used to talk, and not worrying about if it could stay this way... it was just *good.*

Fantastic.

The best damn Christmas in a long time.

After we'd eaten our fill, Derrick walked me back to Night Shift, but didn't come inside – a decision I wrestled with in my head for a while.

Did I *want* to see what the dick was hitting for ten years later?

Of course I did.

But I also wasn't about to get into a repeat performance of my same mistakes.

"This was fun. A *lot* of fun," he said, squeezing my hand as we stopped beside the door.

"I agree."

He nodded, then dipped his head in toward me. "Fun enough that you'll be my New Years' date as well?"

An instant smile bloomed across my face. "I'm sure that can be arranged."

"Good. Consider it settled," he said, then shifted just enough that it only took a slight movement for his lips to press against mine.

Immediately, I was flooded with warmth – all over, but especially between my legs – in a sharp divergence from how freezing cold it was outside.

When we parted ways, I was still smiling – even when a customer on their way out shoulder checked me as I was stepping inside.

I was on too much of a high to be angry, but as I glanced back to at least catch a glimpse of who it was... my eyes went wide.

"*Merry Christmas, cher,*" the stranger said, his ring-covered fingers glittering as he waved.

And then... he was gone.

THE END.

NIGHT SHIFT

To learn more about the Night Shift family, make sure to pick up Equivalent Exchange and Prior Affair in your preferred reading format.

Necessary Departures, Lark's story, is coming in 2023.

If you enjoyed this book, please consider leaving a review at your retailer of choice. It doesn't have to be long - just a line or two about why you enjoyed the book, or even a simple star rating can be very helpful for any author!

Want to stay connected? Text 'CCJRomance' to 74121 or sign up for my newsletter. I'll keep you looped into what I'm doing!

Check out CCJROMANCE.COM for first access to all my new releases, signed paperbacks, merch, and more!

I'm all over the social mediasphere - find me everywhere @beingmrsjones

For a full listing of titles by Christina C Jones, visit www.beingmrsjones.com/books

ABOUT THE AUTHOR

Christina C. Jones is a best-selling romance novelist and digital media creator. A timeless storyteller, she is lauded by readers for her ability to seamlessly weave the complexities of modern life into captivating tales of Black characters in nearly every romance subgenre. In addition to her full-time writing career, she co-founded Girl, Have You Read – a popular digital platform that amplifies Black romance authors and their stories. Christina has a passion for making beautiful things, and be found crafting, cooking, and designing and building a (literal) home with her husband in her spare time.

Made in the USA
Columbia, SC
06 March 2023

13292142R00039